A Note to Parents and Caregivers:

Read-it! Readers are for children who are just starting on the amazing road to reading. These beautiful books support both the acquisition of reading skills and the love of books.

The RED LEVEL presents familiar topics using common words and repeating sentence patterns.
The BLUE LEVEL presents new ideas using a larger vocabulary and varied sentence structure.
The YELLOW LEVEL presents more challenging ideas, a broad vocabulary, and wide variety in sentence structure.

When sharing a book with your child, read in short stretches, pausing often to talk about the pictures. Have your child turn the pages and point to the pictures and familiar words. And be sure to reread favorite stories or parts of stories.

There is no right or wrong way to share books with children. Find time to read with your child and pass on the legacy of literacy.

Adria F. Klein, Ph.D.
Professor Emeritus
California State University
San Bernardino, California

First American edition published in 2003 by
Picture Window Books
5115 Excelsior Boulevard
Suite 232
Minneapolis, MN 55416
1-877-845-8392
www.picturewindowbooks.com

First published in Great Britain by Franklin Watts, 96 Leonard Street, London, EC2A 4XD
Text © Anne Cassidy 2001
Illustration © François Hall 2001

Printed in the United States of America.
1 2 3 4 5 6 08 07 06 05 04 03

Library of Congress Cataloging-in-Publication Data
Cassidy, Anne, 1952-
  Jasper and Jess / written by Anne Cassidy ; illustrated by François Hall.—1st American ed.
    p. cm. — (Read-it! readers)
  Summary: Jasper the dog and Jess the cat are enemies who growl and hiss at each other
every day as Jasper chases Jess out of the garden, but the day Jess gets stuck on the roof,
Jasper is the only one who can help her.
  ISBN 1-4048-0061-1
  [1. Dogs—Fiction. 2. Cats—Fiction. 3. Friendship—Fiction.] I. Hall, François, ill. II. Title. III.
Series.
  PZ7.C26857 Jas 2003
  [E]—dc21   2002074920

PICTURE WINDOW BOOKS

Jasper
and Jess

Written by Anne Cassidy

Illustrated by François Hall

Reading Advisors:
Adria F. Klein, Ph.D.
Professor Emeritus, California State University
San Bernardino, California

Ruth Thomas
Durham Public Schools
Durham, North Carolina

R. Ernice Bookout
Durham Public Schools
Durham, North Carolina

Picture Window Books
Minneapolis, Minnesota

Jasper and Jess were enemies.

Jasper liked to chase Jess
out of the yard.

Every day, Jasper waited
until Jess came outside.

He chased her until she ran up the apple tree.

He barked and growled at her.

She arched her back and
hissed at him.

One day Jess didn't appear.

Jasper looked for her
behind the bushes and
in the flowerbeds.

He looked in the

rock garden

and over the fence.

But Jess wasn't there.

Then Jasper heard a sound.
He looked up at the house.

Jess was stuck on the roof!

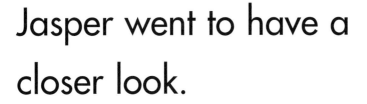

Jasper went to have a
closer look.

Jess was hanging down
from the gutter!

Jasper ran up and down
the yard, barking.

But no one heard him.

He scratched at the back door.

But no one was at home.

Quickly, he pulled a lawn
chair over to the house.

"Jump onto the chair, Jess!"
he shouted.

Jess was frightened but she closed her eyes and let go.

It was a long way down.

Jess fell through the air
and landed on the chair.

She was safe!

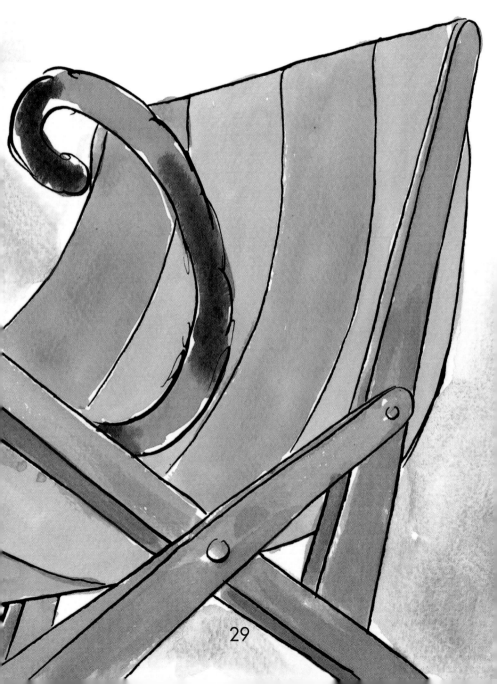

Jasper was glad he had helped Jess.

Now he could chase her out of the yard again!

Red Level

The Best Snowman, by Margaret Nash 1-4048-0048-4
Bill's Baggy Pants, by Susan Gates 1-4048-0050-6
Cleo and Leo, by Anne Cassidy 1-4048-0049-2
Felix on the Move, by Maeve Friel 1-4048-0055-7
Jasper and Jess, by Anne Cassidy 1-4048-0061-1
The Lazy Scarecrow, by Jillian Powell 1-4048-0062-X
Little Joe's Big Race, by Andy Blackford 1-4048-0063-8
The Little Star, by Deborah Nash 1-4048-0065-4
The Naughty Puppy, by Jillian Powell 1-4048-0067-0
Selfish Sophie, by Damian Kelleher 1-4048-0069-7

Blue Level

The Bossy Rooster, by Margaret Nash 1-4048-0051-4
Jack's Party, by Ann Bryant 1-4048-0060-3
Little Red Riding Hood, by Maggie Moore 1-4048-0064-6
Recycled!, by Jillian Powell 1-4048-0068-9
The Sassy Monkey, by Anne Cassidy 1-4048-0058-1
The Three Little Pigs, by Maggie Moore 1-4048-0071-9

Yellow Level

Cinderella, by Barrie Wade 1-4048-0052-2
The Crying Princess, by Anne Cassidy 1-4048-0053-0
Eight Enormous Elephants, by Penny Dolan 1-4048-0054-9
Freddie's Fears, by Hilary Robinson 1-4048-0056-5
Goldilocks and the Three Bears, by Barrie Wade 1-4048-0057-3
Mary and the Fairy, by Penny Dolan 1-4048-0066-2
Jack and the Beanstalk, by Maggie Moore 1-4048-0059-X
The Three Billy Goats Gruff, by Barrie Wade 1-4048-0070-0